The Magic Plum Tree

BASED ON A TALE FROM THE JATAKA

BY **Freya Littledale**

ILLUSTRATED BY **Enrico Arno**

Crown Publishers, Inc. New York

Text copyright © 1981 by Freya Littledale
Illustrations copyright © 1981 by Enrico Arno
All rights reserved. No part of this publication may be reproduced,
stored in a retrieval system, or transmitted, in any form or by any means,
electronic, mechanical, photocopying, recording, or otherwise, without
prior written permission of the publisher. Inquiries should be addressed
to Crown Publishers, Inc., One Park Avenue, New York, New York 10016
Manufactured in the United States of America
Published simultaneously in Canada by General Publishing Company Limited
10 9 8 7 6 5 4 3 2 1

The text of this book is set in 16 point Plantin.
The illustrations are black half-tone drawings with separations,
prepared by the artist, for green, red, and brown.

Library of Congress Cataloging in Publication Data

Littledale, Freya, 1929-
    The magic plum tree.

    Summary: Because each of the three princes sees the
plum tree at a different season, he forms a different
impression of what it looks like.
    1. Jataka stories, English. [1. Seasons—Fiction.
2. Trees—Fiction. 3. Princes—Fiction. 4. Jataka
stories] I. Arno, Enrico. II. Title.
BQ1462.E5L57 1981   [E]   81-2857
ISBN 0-517-54166-1   AACR2

For Beatrice de Regniers

Once upon a time there was a wise king
who had three young sons.
They lived in a castle by the sea.
The princes saw the sea, sand, and sky.
They saw wild geese and palm trees.
But everything looked the same to them,
day after day after day.
One morning the king took his eldest son
for a ride in his chariot.
They rode up a mountain,
into a forest,
and along a lake.

The prince saw many trees,
but one was more beautiful
than all the rest.
"What kind of tree is that?" he asked.
"It is a plum tree," said the king.
The prince touched a leaf,
and it fell to the ground.
Then a warm breeze blew,
and leaves filled the air.
"It is beautiful!" said the prince.
"Yes it is," said the king.
And they rode back to the castle by the sea.

The prince ran to find his brothers.
"I saw a plum tree!" he said.

"We want to see it too!" they cried.

And they went to tell the king.

"It isn't fair, that only he
should see the tree."
The king stroked his beard,

and puffed on his pipe.

"You must wait a few months."

And that was all he said.

The princes studied their lessons
and played their flutes.

They flew their kites
and found shells in the sand.

Winter came,
and the king took his second son
for a ride in the chariot.
They rode up the mountain,
into the forest,
and along the lake.
There the prince saw the tree.
Its branches were brown and bare.
"Is that the plum tree?" asked the prince.
"Yes," said the king.
The prince touched the cold, wet bark
and turned away.
"I don't like it," he said.
"That's all right," said the king.

And they rode back to the castle by the sea.

The prince ran to find his brothers.

"The plum tree is ugly!" he said.

"It is beautiful!" said the eldest.

"I want to see it for myself," said the youngest.

And he went to tell the king.

"You must wait a few months," said the king.

And that was all he said.

The princes read their books
and painted pictures.

They watched dancers act out stories
to the beating of the drums.

When spring came
the king took his youngest son
for a ride in the chariot.

They rode up the mountain,
into the forest,
and along the lake.

The prince saw many trees,
but one stood out from all the rest.
"Is that the plum tree?" he asked.
"Yes," said the king.
The prince touched the soft white blossoms
and looked up at the sky through the branches.
"It is wonderful!" he said.
"I agree," said the king.
And they rode back to the castle by the sea.

The prince ran to find his brothers.

"I saw the plum tree," he said.

"It is covered with blossoms."

"It is not!" said the middle prince.

"The plum tree is bare."

"You are both wrong," said the eldest.

"It is covered with leaves."

"Well," said the youngest prince,

"perhaps we did not see the same tree.

Let us ask our father."

But all the king said was, "Wait."

Summer came.

The sun was like fire in the sky.

The princes swam and fished
and sailed their toy boats in the sea.

Then early one morning
the king took his three sons
for a ride in the chariot.
They rode up the mountain,

into the forest,

and along the lake.

And there they saw the tree.

Its branches were heavy with deep red plums.

"Is this the tree I saw?"
  asked the youngest prince.
"Yes," said the king.
"You have all seen this tree,
  but you have seen it with different eyes,
  in different seasons."
"I can't believe it," said the middle prince.
"I can," said the eldest.
"Let us taste the plums," said the youngest.
  The princes each picked a plum
  and sat down beneath the tree.
  Then they ate the ripe red fruit
  while a bird sang in the branches.

AUTHOR'S NOTE

The Magic Plum Tree is based on a tale (No. 248)
in *The Jataka, or Stories of the Buddha's Former
Births* (vol. II, Professor E. B. Cowell, ed., Cambridge
University Press, 1895). *The Jataka,* part of the
sacred literature of Buddhism, dates from before
the third century B.C., and is among the richest
and most important sources of folklore.